Ambrose
and the
Cathedral Dream

Margo Sorenson
illustrated by
Katalin Szegedi

Ambrose the Mouse

LITURGICAL PRESS
Collegeville, Minnesota

www.litpress.org

mbrose lined up with his mouse cousins.

"One! Two! Over you go!" Grandpa shouted.

Ambrose clenched his paws and squeezed his eyes shut.

All the mice tumbled into somersaults across the cathedral floor.

All—except Ambrose.

SPLAT!

"Ouch!" he squeaked, rubbing his nose.

"Ha, ha!" hooted his little cousins. "Hee, hee!"

"Ambrose goofed again!" his cousin Nicholas snickered. "Just like always!"

Ambrose twitched his whiskers angrily.

From the corner of his eye, Ambrose caught a sympathetic glance from his cousin Emma. He swiped at his nose with a paw and sighed.

Grandpa frowned and scolded, "Ambrose, practice your somersaults! Or else you can't help the rest of us build the cathedral!"

"Tsk, tsk, Ambrose, dear," murmured Grandma.

Ambrose stared at the stone floor.

Grandpa sighed. "You've been daydreaming again, instead of practicing."

"Ambrose will *never* help to build the cathedral!" his cousin Simon tittered.

"He stares into space!" said Ulric.

"He's a nobody!" said Gilbert.

"No, he's not," Emma whispered. But no one heard.

"He can't do *anything*!" said Geoffrey, another cousin.

"Except daydream!" a sixth cousin snickered.

Ambrose's cousins rolled on the cathedral floor, laughing. Emma shook her head.

Ambrose's pink nose wiggled. "I *can* do something." He glared at his cousins. "And I *do* practice my somersaults."

Well, *sometimes*. He daydreamed more than he practiced, he admitted to himself.

He daydreamed about how beautiful the finished cathedral would be.

He daydreamed how he would help William the Master Builder to build it.

And he imagined all his mouse cousins cheering for him.

"You're special, Ambrose!" they would shout.

"Pay attention, Ambrose," Grandpa said.

Ambrose blinked.

Grandma looked at Ambrose. "Remember, our work is important. For many years, our mouse family has somersaulted to help build the cathedral," she said, pointing into the cathedral nave. "Watch!"

The cousins looked. Ambrose did, too.

One of the workmen building the pulpit leaned against a fluted pillar. His eyes began to flutter. He yawned. His hammering grew slower.

Kachunk. Ka-chunk. Ka—

"Now!" Grandpa commanded. Gilbert, Simon, and Nicholas scooted across the stone floor. They lined up in front of the workman. Together, they turned perfect somersaults and raced back to safety.

"Eh?" The workman blinked. He sat up straight. "What was that?" He glanced around him. He shook his head.

He grasped the hammer and set to work.

KaCHUNK! KaCHUNK!

All the cousins cheered and clapped.

Grandpa looked at Ambrose over his spectacles. "Do you see how our somersaults surprise the workmen and keep them awake so they can build? You must practice those somersaults if you want to help, Ambrose."

The mouse cousins began giggling and choking with laughter, wriggling around on the floor again.

"Ambrose help? Hee, hee!"

"Ambrose somersault? Ha, ha!"

Ambrose squeezed his eyes shut. He wanted to clap his paws over his ears.

"Yes, I will!" Ambrose burst out. "But—I'll do more than all of you! I—I'm going to help William the Master Builder, *himself*!"

The mouse cousins stopped giggling. They all stared at Ambrose.

Grandpa raised his eyebrows. "Hmmmm," he said. "William *himself*?" He shook his head. "Well, if that is *really* your dream—" Grandpa paused, "maybe you *could* help William. After all, I helped Gregory, his father, when he was the Master Builder."

Ambrose's eyes widened. "I— I *could* help William? How?" Ambrose asked. He clasped his paws together.

"How? You must find out for yourself," Grandpa said. He and Grandma exchanged glances. "But—the Master Builder always has a dream, too," he said with a mysterious smile. "If you help him find *his* dream, then, you can help him. So, practice, will you?"

Ambrose's heart beat faster. *He* would help William find his dream!

Ambrose practiced his somersaults every day next to the choir stalls. He got bruises and bumps. He got aches and lumps. But he kept practicing. Emma helped him keep count.

Each day, Ambrose followed William the Master Builder as he checked up on the workmen.

Ambrose heard William sigh, "When will I find my dream?"

But William didn't say what his dream was.

How could he help? Ambrose frowned. William was never sleepy. How could a somersault help him?

At first, Ambrose hoped William's dream might be that all the huge stones for building the cathedral would be hauled from the ships in the harbor to the cathedral site. But after all the giant stones were unloaded, Ambrose heard William murmur again, "When will it happen?"

Maybe, Ambrose decided, when the flying buttresses were done, that would be the answer. Ambrose could see the frames of the flying buttresses soaring high above the ground, now, almost finished. But William only sighed while he walked among the piles of lumber and stone on the cathedral floor.

Hiding in one of the chapels, Ambrose watched the glass-makers join the sparkling glass shapes together with lead strips. The stained glass windows would send many-colored beams of light flooding into the cathedral. But William just frowned and folded his arms, watching them work.

Metal workers hammered out ornamental bolts and locks and hinges for the cathedral doors. Once the doors were finished and the people came into the cathedral to worship, would William get what he wanted? Ambrose asked himself. But William didn't say a word about the doors.

One night, after the workmen left for the day, Grandma and Grandpa brought the mouse cousins to gaze at the beautiful altar that was almost finished. William never said anything about the altar, either. Ambrose sighed.

The weeks passed. The mice raced across the stone floor to their somersaulting work. Ambrose scampered through the transept, dodging among the fluted pillars, following William, and hoping. Emma tagged along behind him.

Ambrose watched William check on the carpenters working on the tall spire, which would rise above the roof and reach toward the heavens when the cathedral was finished. Then he sneaked past some of the workmen carving the baptismal font. Ambrose winced. He'd have to watch out that his cousins didn't push him in for a surprise swim, once it was filled.

Other workmen toiled on the funny-looking gargoyles. The gargoyles scared him when he ran into them by accident in the middle of the night, as he secretly watched his mouse cousins play moonlight tag together—without him.

Ambrose crouched behind William near the pulpit, with its curved staircase.

"The cathedral will be so beautiful. But—if only I could find my dream," William sighed.

Just then, Ambrose's tail twitched. It rolled a huge nail across the floor. William turned away from the carpenters to pick up the nail.

There, in plain sight, was Ambrose! A beam of sunlight through a vacant clerestory window shimmered on his fur.

"What's *this*?" William exclaimed. "A mouse?"

Ambrose froze. Help! What could he do? A somersault—would a somersault surprise William enough so Ambrose could escape?

Now! Ambrose told himself. Would all his practice pay off?

He saw Emma peek out from behind a pillar, her eyes wide.

He had to do it!

Whoops! Paws over tail, Ambrose somersaulted.

"A *somersault*?" William the Master Builder exclaimed. "A somersault," he repeated slowly. "When I was a boy—." He stopped. A light shone in his eyes. "I *do* remember a mouse," he said softly. Then a grin spread across his face. "Stay, little one. Don't run away. Maybe *you* can help me find my dream!"

Ambrose's heart almost stopped.

"I'll be back," William said.

Ambrose watched William walk away. Yes! Now he could run to safety!

Wait. Ambrose's heart pounded. William said that maybe *Ambrose* could help him!

Grandpa's voice echoed in his ears. "You will help him, just as I helped Gregory, his father."

Ambrose could hear his mouse cousins making fun of him. "You'll never help William! You'll never get your dream! You're nobody!" they had jeered. Only Emma had believed in him.

All right. He had to stay here.

Emma peeked from her hiding place. "Stay, Ambrose!" she whispered.

Ambrose gave her a shaky smile, but he quivered with fright.

Then, William came back. A young boy came with him.

"This is my son, Gregory," William said, "named after my father, Gregory the Master Builder. My dream is that my son will help me build the cathedral, just as I helped my father."

The dream! Ambrose squeezed his paws together in excitement. But how could he help?

"Gregory has always been too busy daydreaming and playing." William smiled at Gregory. "I told him a mouse at the cathedral could do a somersault. Maybe he will want to help me, too—as long as *you* are around to play with him."

"Can he do the somersault again, Father?" Gregory asked.

Yes! Ambrose almost squeaked aloud. Yes! I *can* help William the Master Builder!

And Ambrose took three deep breaths, stuck out his paws, and turned the best somersault ever.

"Oh, Father!" Gregory exclaimed. "Imagine working in a cathedral with a little mouse who can turn somersaults! Maybe I will stay and help you!"

Emma skipped joyfully in a little circle next to one of the chapels.

Ambrose felt his nose turn pink with happiness. Wait until he told his mouse cousins—and Grandma and Grandpa!

Grandpa! Ambrose's eyes opened wide. Was it Grandpa who somersaulted in front of William when William was a little boy? Was that why William agreed to help his own father Gregory build the cathedral?

Behind him, Ambrose heard squeaking and cheering.

"Yeah, Ambrose!"

"You did it!"

"You're special!"

He turned around. All his mouse cousins were lined up in the shadows in front of the choir stalls, clapping their paws, led by Emma.

And there was Grandpa, smiling and wiping his spectacles, and Grandma, dabbing at her eyes with the corner of her apron.

Ambrose's heart lifted suddenly. He looked up at the graceful cathedral spire reaching toward the sky.

Now *he* was really going to help build the cathedral, too.

For my dear family—Jim, Jane and Chris, Jill and Matt

For Dr. Bryce Lyon and Father Cyril Gorman, O.S.B.

—*Margo Sorenson*

Ambrose the Mouse welcomes correspondence at margo@margosorenson.com or through Liturgical Press, Saint John's Abbey, at the address below.

Art direction and design by Ann Blattner

Illustrations: © 2006 by Katalin Szegedi

1 2 3 4 5 6 7 8 9

Sorenson, Margo.
        Ambrose and the cathedral dream / Margo Sorenson ; illustrated by Katalin Szegedi.
            p. cm. — (Ambrose the mouse books)
        Summary: Ambrose, a young mouse, must put aside his daydreaming in order to master the art of somersaulting and to help complete the building of the grand cathedral.
        ISBN-13: 978-0-8146-3004-4 (alk. paper)
        ISBN-10: 0-8146-3004-9 (alk. paper)
        [1. Mice—Fiction.   2. Building—Fiction.   3. Dreams—Fiction.   4. Cathedrals—Fiction.
    5. Determination (Personality trait)—Fiction.   6. Self-confidence—Fiction.]   I. Szegedi, Katalin, 1963– ill.   II. Title.   III. Series: Sorenson, Margo. Ambrose the mouse books.

PZ7.S72147Am 2006
[E]—dc22

2004026404